Christmas in the Barn

BY MARGARET WISE BROWN

PICTURES BY BARBARA COONEY

NEW YORK *Thomas Y. Crowell Company*

CHRISTMAS IN THE BARN

IN A big warm barn
In an ancient field

The oxen lowed,
The donkey squealed,
The horses stomped,
The cattle sighed,

And quietly the daylight died
In the sunset of the west.
And a star rose
Brighter than all stars in the sky.

The field mice scampered in the hay

And two people who had lost their way
Walked into the barn at the end of the day
And they were allowed to sleep in the hay
"Because there was no room in the inn."

The little mice rustled in the sweet dry grass
Near the lambs and the kine and the ox
and the ass.

The horses pawed the golden straw,

The little donkey brayed "Hee Haw,"

And there they were
All safe and warm
All together in that ancient barn
When hail—
  The first wail
  Of a newborn babe reached the night
  Where one great star was burning bright
  And shepherds with their sheep
  Are come to watch him sleep.

What child is this
Who is born here
Where the oxen stomp and peer,

STAR BRIGHT

Away in a manger
No crib for his bed
What child is this
Who lays down his sweet head?

In the big warm barn
In the ancient field
The little child sleeps,
The donkey squeals

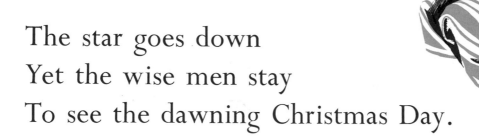

The star goes down
Yet the wise men stay
To see the dawning Christmas Day.

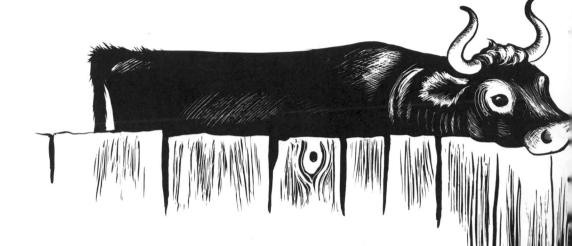

The child was sleeping in the hay
And there they were
All safe and warm
All together in that ancient barn.